BEADLE, JONES, EVETT ~ HACKFORT & TEARLE

for JONNY, ISLA & JACKSON

CLARION BOOKS   3 PARK AVENUE
NEW YORK, NEW YORK, 10016

COPYRIGHT © 2016 BY MEG McLAREN

FIRST PUBLISHED IN THE UNITED KINGDOM
IN 2016 BY ANDERSEN PRESS.

PUBLISHED IN THE UNITED STATES IN 2017.

THE TEXT
WAS SET IN
AGED BOOK.

THE ILLUSTRATIONS IN
THIS BOOK WERE DONE
USING DIGITAL MEDIA.

LIBRARY OF CONGRESS CATALOGING-IN-PUBLICATION DATA IS AVAILABLE

ISBN 978-0-544-78469-7

4500562622   Manufactured in China

STAGE DOOR ▶

STA
DO

RABBIT MAGIC

MEG McLAREN

~CLARION BOOKS~

HOUGHTON MIFFLIN HARCOURT ★ BOSTON NEW YORK

The hardest part of any magic show is picking the right assistant.

Not everyone is a born performer.

Some suffer from stage fright,

while others have a terrible sense of timing.

And not everyone understands props.

But Houdini the rabbit was a natural.

TA-DA A!

He loved magic.

And he had a knack for bringing the team together.

Helping the crew relax . . .

A CARROT
A DAY KEEPS THE
EYE DOCTOR AWAY

RAWK!
RAWK!

Performing the
pre-show checks . . .

PAWS
OFF

YUCK!

Houdini took care of everyone and everything.

So one night
when things
went wrong . . .

AAH!

Houdini went on with the show.

AAAAH!

OOH...

The crowd thought it was the best trick ever.

But the magician wasn't too pleased . . .

when they discovered his new role might be permanent.

As rehearsals got underway, not everyone
was impressed by Houdini's talent.

YUM

And the new boss was
always far too busy.

INTRODUCING...

HOUDINI

But word soon spread.

Houdini's hard work began to pay off
as people flocked to see the show.

 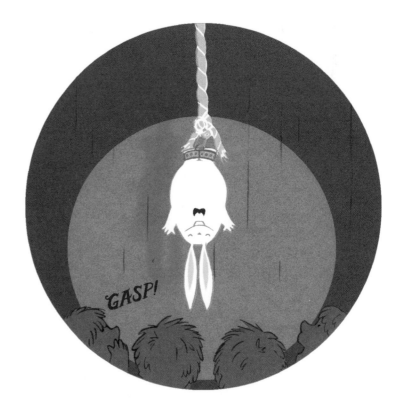

TICK
TICK
TICK

The more daring
his tricks became,
the more the crowd
loved him.

Houdini was a hit.

TA-DAA

HOORAY!

GASP!

Night after night the audience cheered.

Clap Clap CLAP CLAP CLAP Clap Clap CLAP CLAP Clap CLAP Clap CLAP Clap CLAP CLAP CLAP Clap Clap CLAP CLAP Clap clap clap CLAP CLAP Clap CLAP CLAP CLAP CLAP

But for Houdini, the
excitement was fading.

Though Houdini had enjoyed being the star of the show,

someone else needed the spotlight more.

So he gathered
the team together.
On the last night
of his sold-out tour,
Houdini would attempt . . .

his
greatest
trick.

TA-DAAA!
TA-DAA!
TA-DAA!
Ta-daa!
WOOHOO!
ORAY!
CLAP
GASP!
CLAP
CLAP
CLAP

Which goes to show

that sometimes rabbits
(and people)

do the most unexpected things—

because life is truly magical when you share it.

SOLD OUT

FEATURING
HOUDINI
AND THE
HOPPERS

STAGE
DOOR

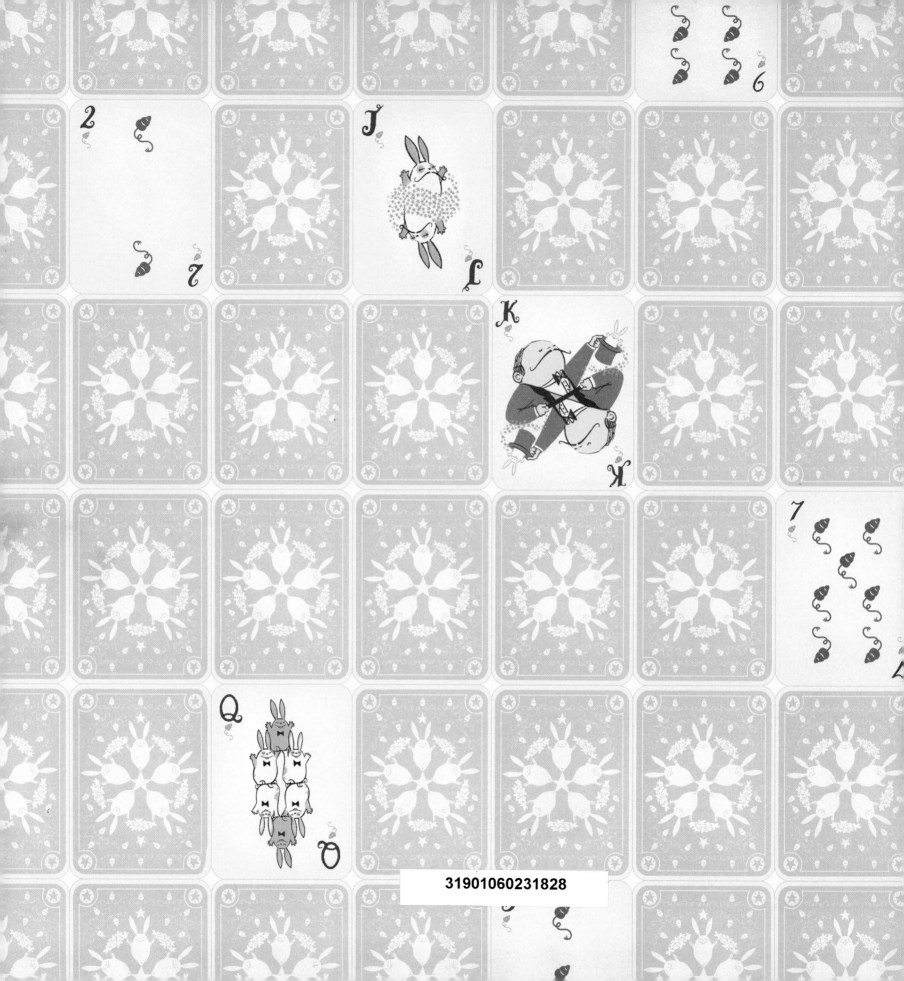